To Quin,
my favorite little monster,
and to Theo,
who started all this nonsense.

Even fantasy creatures and monsters start out as adorable tiny babies, and as every parent knows, babies present unique challenges.

For starters, have you ever had to put a diaper on a baby with a tail... or nine?

Unicorn foals are capable
of farting rainbows and sparkles
within an hour of being born.

Teething werewolf cubs
can be a beast of a problem.

Baby dragons really put those
'flame-resistant' clothing labels to the test.

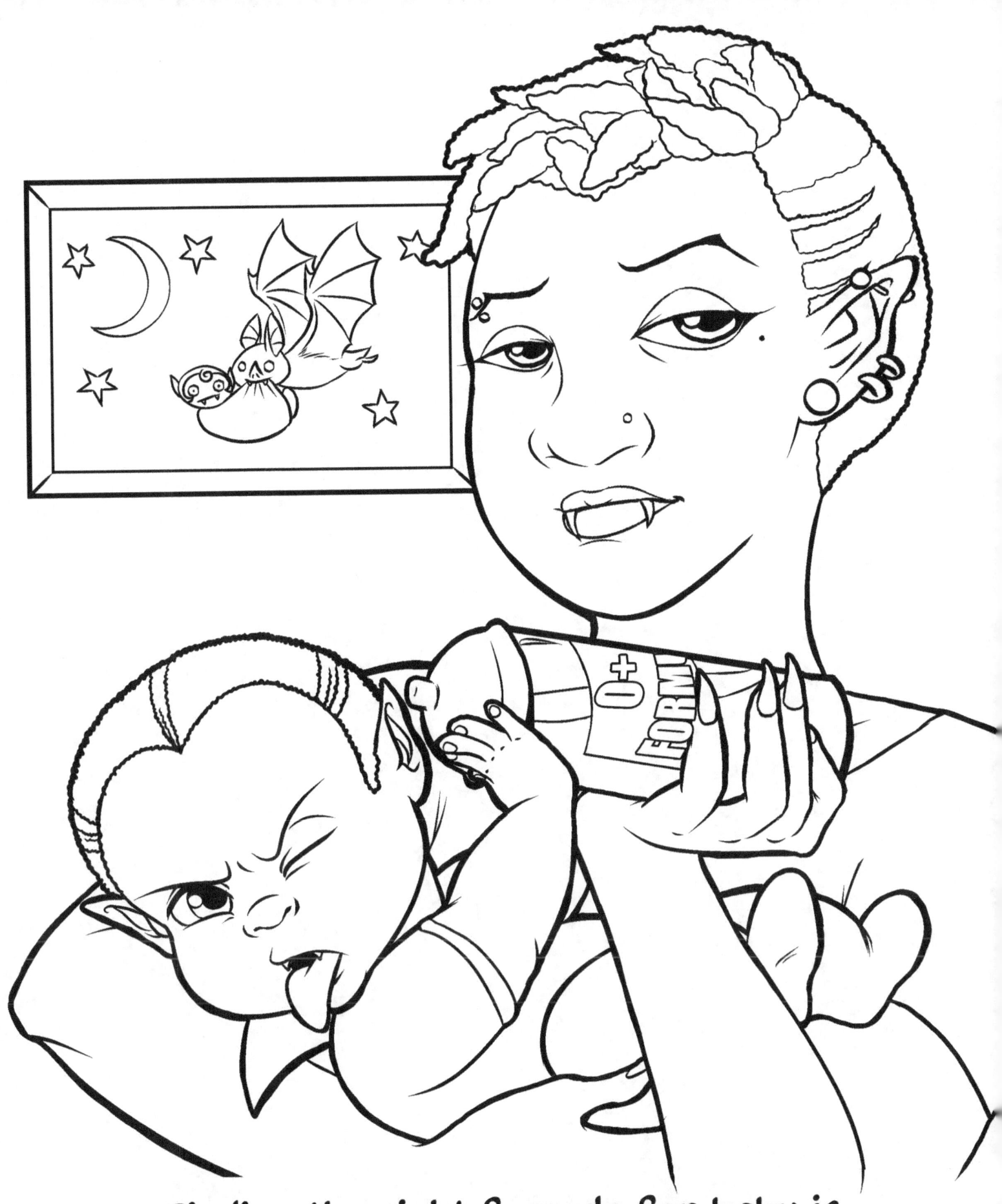

Finding the right formula for baby is
hard enough without having
to choose a blood type.

Baby griffins are not nearly as
majestic or intimidating when freshly hatched.

It takes a lot of yarn
to knit Bigfoot baby booties.

If you ever thought babies learning to walk were awkward, just try teaching them to fly.

One might assume that living underwater
would make it easier to keep baby clean.
(One would be mistaken.)

Minotaurs need to take
special precautions when they bring
their calves to labyrinthine malls.

It's hard to solve deadly riddles
when your sphinx can only manage baby talk.

Even baby yetis need to be bundled up
against the cold.

Gorgons and basilisks have to find
creative solutions for play dates.
Staring contests are not advised.

With three heads, chimera cubs produce
triple-volume tantrums.

Even massive, city-destroying monsters
need to start small.

While every parent fears the worst happening to their child, for a phoenix it just means having to start over and over again.

Maria "Pip" Lorimer is a parent, an artist,
and a lifelong fan of fantasy creatures.
They are raising their own little monster,
known as Q-bear, in Minnesota.